# AFTER THE FALL

ALSO BY VICTORIA ROBERTS

*Cattitudes*

*Australia Felix*

*Biographees*

*My Day*

# W. W. NORTON & COMPANY

*New York  London*

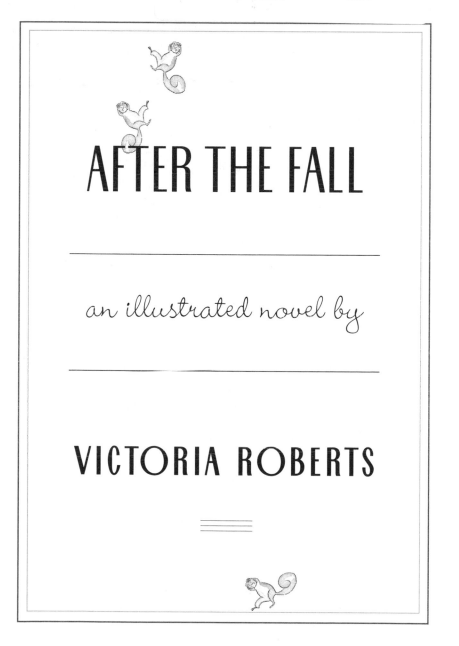

# AFTER THE FALL

*an illustrated novel by*

## VICTORIA ROBERTS

Copyright © 2013 by Victoria Roberts

For information about permission to reproduce selections from
this book, write to Permissions, W. W. Norton & Company, Inc.,
500 Fifth Avenue, New York, NY 10110

For information about special discounts for bulk purchases, please contact
W. W. Norton Special Sales at specialsales@wwnorton.com or 800-233-4830

Manufacturing by Courier Westford
Book design by Barbara Bachman
Production manager: Julia Druskin

Library of Congress Cataloging-in-Publication Data

Roberts, Victoria, 1957–
After the fall : an illustrated novel / by Victoria Roberts. — 1st ed.
p. cm.
ISBN 978-0-393-07355-3 (hardcover)
1. Graphic novels.  I. Title.
PN6727.R568A37 2012
741.5'973—dc23
2012023516

W. W. Norton & Company, Inc.
500 Fifth Avenue, New York, N.Y. 10110
www.wwnorton.com

W. W. Norton & Company Ltd.
Castle House, 75/76 Wells Street, London W1T 3QT

1 2 3 4 5 6 7 8 9 0

for Joanne
Martin

Map

Olive

Phoebe

Sancho

Gudelia

Usvelia

DRAMATIS PERSONAE

Mother

Pops

Alan

Sis

# AFTER THE FALL

# CHAPTER
## 1

"Pops won't sell the Olmec head!" My little sister, Alexandra, greeted me at the door when I arrived home from the Lycée. So did our three pugs.

"Mom says Pops won't sell

the Olmec head and we're ruined! She wants to see you,
Alan. Pops wants to see you, too." I set down my schoolbag and walked down the parquet floor to Mother's room.

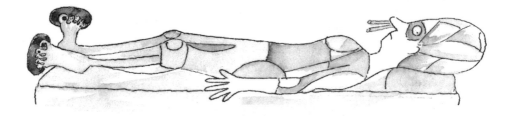

Mother was in creams. She had two straws coming out of her nose to make sure her airways were clear.

"*Ahorita no puede hablar tu mami, m'hijito, se está haciendo su trata-miento,*" or, "Your mother can't talk right now, she's having her beauty treatment, my son," said Gudelia, closely guarding Mother's door.

Gudelia, our cook, raised us in Spanish. We have Mexican accents. Mother was born in Buenos Aires and doesn't like the way we speak.

It was my job to walk the pugs at four. I took them across the street to Central Park, to Cedar Hill where they met up with their pal Vivienne Li, a black pug, Vivi for short.

When I came home I went straight to Pops's study. He was in his pajamas and paisley robe reading the *Times*. He had just gotten up.

Usvelia, Gudelia's sister and our housekeeper, had man-
aged to vacuum around him, and was leaving.

"*¿No se te antoja un Choco Milk, m'hijito?*" or, "Wouldn't you like a chocolate milk, my son?" she asked, dragging the vacuum cleaner behind her.

"*No, gracias,*" I replied.

Pops sat quietly for a moment, which made me think he had forgotten I was in the room.

"You wanted to talk to me, Pops?" I was not afraid of Pops. He was too absent-minded to ever get too angry.

"Is school over already?" He seemed surprised.

"It's half past four, Pops."

"Oh, so it is. We've lost everything, Alan," said Pops finally, his head still buried in the newspaper. "Never put all of your eggs in one basket. Even the basket is gone."

I tried to get more out of him, but his only reply was, "What is there to understand about everything being gone? When it's gone, it's gone!"

Pops, an inventor, had made us filthy rich, so how could we suddenly be so poor?

I helped Sis with her homework: France and the Gauls.
Sis had the appropriate hairdo.

"Why are you in trouble, bubble?" she asked, too clever
for her years. She's only seven, three years my junior.

"I forgot to bring home the permission slip for the
excursion to the Barnes Collection for Mother to sign to
give to Monsieur Le Becq," was my disappointing reply. I
didn't have the heart to tell her we were poor.

After dinner, Sis had her bath and I took my shower.

Mother and Pops were too busy arguing to say good-
night to us, so I tucked Sis in.

"It's the end," said Sis. "I
know all about the new poverty.
It's dire." Sis loved using a new
word.

FROM THIS    TO THIS

All I could pick up from the
argument down the hall was
that our demise was due to a
sudden regime change in China.

"Yes, let's blame everything on China!' shouted Mother,
and then a door slammed.

When Gudelia saw that my light was still on, she poked
her head in the door.

"*No te preocupes, m'hijito, no pasa nada,*" she said.

So it was true. Gudelia only says
everything is going to be all right when
things are inevitably bad, like when we
go for an injection, or when I had the
revolting treatment for sinusitis, or
when our old blind pug
Silka fell off the pent-
house balcony.

I lay in bed with my
eyes open. "I'll work at
Schrafft's," was my last
thought before I fell into
a restless sleep.

# CHAPTER 2

The next morning I awoke in Central Park. Everything was in its usual place, only out-of-doors, with trees growing in the middle of what now was the living room, dining room, and other rooms.

Gudelia served breakfast alfresco by the Kerbs Memo-
rial Boathouse.

"We don't have to go to school!" cried Sis.

"You won't be welcome at the Lycée," Mother addressed me, blowing cigarette smoke through her nose. "Your father hasn't sent in the tuition fees."

She looked so sad.

Mother was either UP or

D
O
W
N.

I couldn't bear it when she was down, so I put on my school uniform—which Gudelia had laid out—picked up my schoolbag, and headed "for school."

At three thirty I came "home" to the park.

Mother greeted me in the Glade, now our foyer, with a voluminous hug.

"How was school, darling? You mean to say they let you in? Marvelous!"

She was UP.

Pops was in his study, a dark spot between the boat-house and Fifth Avenue, behind the café. He sat on the

ground where it sloped at a similar angle to his own easy chair at home. All of his books were stacked against the wall, as they had been at home.

He had had a good day, probably because he got some daylight for a change. He started pacing up and down his room. There was no hope of a conversation when he was that deep in thought, so I exited, though we hadn't any doors.

I visited Mother instead in her room, which was directly across from Pops's study, on a hill overlooking Conservatory Water, where she could keep an eye on things—the perfect lookout.

I helped Mother
strategically place the
plastic-covered clothes
rack on wheels that
housed her wardrobe
to block the view of the
Alice in Wonderland
statue, which she con-
sidered grotesque.

"Perfect!" cried Mother, running down the hill toward
the pond. "And look what Gudelia did for me!"

Sitting beside the pond was our turquoise Chinese porcelain foo dog, a white cord tied around its neck and submerged in the water. Mother retrieved the cord, and tied to the end of it was a bottle of Impériale by Guerlain. She loved to put on cool cologne. She always kept a bar fridge in her bathroom.

"Ice cold!" Mother splashed cologne about her ears and

neck, and put a dab on my nose with her fingertip. "Where would this family be without Usvelia and Gudelia?"

Usvelia and Gudelia, who had lived in, now lived out, commuting to and from their home in Queens. They had left for the day.

Sis was nowhere to be found. I headed up the hill to her wing, south of the pond just below the exit to Fifth Avenue at 72nd Street. I found her dolls, her books, her bear, her Creepy Crawlers oven, but no Sis.

"Hey kids, come to Acapulco!" cried Mother from the sandbox next to the ladies' bathrooms. She was sitting on a banana lounge reading the September *Vogue*, sipping a margarita.

Sis appeared, her face white as a sheet. She had spent the day with a mime who taught her how to be a living statue.

"I suppose we have to start thinking about dinner. Are you kids hungry? Get dressed!" Mother squinted in Sis's direction. "What *is* that gunk on your face, Alex?"

We dressed for dinner, in layers.

Mother, Sis, and I sat opposite the pond in semi-darkness. At 5:26 p.m. lamps came on across the pond, but not on our side.

"We'll have to shoot some swans," said Mother, glaring at two birds floating in the pond, barely visible now that it was darker. "Did your Pops bring a gun?"

"No, I didn't bring a gun." Pops emerged from his study. He had on several layers, like us, but they were all pajamas, and two satin robes on top of that.

"Oh, shoot!" said Mother. "I'll just have to strangle them with my bare hands." She put down her margarita glass and disappeared into the darkness.

"I think they're geese, not swans," said Pops, unperturbed.

"I'm a vegetarian!" cried Sis, who given the choice would live on peanut M&Ms.

Eight minutes later Mother returned carrying two giant swans, one under each arm, made out of aluminum foil, like the swans they give you in restaurants when you take home leftovers, only much bigger.

"Monsieur Marcel?" Pops asked Mother, who nodded.

Mother unwrapped the contents of the swans. There were fried cheese balls covered in breadcrumbs for Sis,

*coq au vin* for Mother, grilled *rognons* (veal kidneys) for me,
*cassoulet* for Pops, and a strawberry *bavarois* for dessert.

Monsieur Marcel was the maître d' at Le Château
Bohème, one of Pops's restaurants. Pops disappeared
momentarily and returned with a bottle of Bordeaux.

Over dinner Pops reiterated that we had lost everything and that the meal was "charity."

Mother, who only used the word "charity" in a sentence if it was accompanied by the word "ball," had another glass of red wine.

At 6:26 p.m. the lamps came on on our side of the pond, and it was almost too bright for dessert.

# CHAPTER
# 3

Why didn't we stay with relatives?
Mother had fought with them all.
Uncle Bobby
had the wrong
idea about how
to defog the
car windows.
Their relation-
ship ended on
a road trip to
the Rockies.

Aunt Delia was "a leech," Uncle Frank was "too tall." And so on.

"Blood is thicker than water," Pops would say, and Mother would reply, "So's maple syrup."

Some of the relationships were restored, but were never quite the same.

After dinner, Sis retired to the north wing, Mother to the south wing, and Pops to his study, southeast of the pond.

My room was further away, east of Cedar Hill, close to the exit at 79th Street. I had walked past this spot daily with the pugs in broad daylight and thought nothing of it. Tonight, however, I went to my quarters escorted by my

electric car because I'm afraid of rats. I'm also afraid of a raccoon Sis said lives behind the ladies' toilets.

"It sunbathes on the roof of the café," she told me. "It's huge!"

The electric car was a toy vintage Porsche powered by a flashlight. It was a prize from Mother for getting three gold medals and a *Diplôme d'honneur* at the Lycée last year.

Sis, who came to F. A. O. Schwartz when I picked it out, said it was a piece of junk and encouraged me to go for a tent instead. She was right. It didn't work, ever.

Mother made no effort to return or exchange it, exclaiming, "Well, you made your choice, and you must learn to live with your choices. I certainly have!"

Pops made a new motor for it. He is a genius. (Well, maybe not a financial genius.)

Pops invented Smokos, the cigarette that isn't a cigarette, and cured almost everybody in the world of the nicotine habit. That's how we got to live in a penthouse on Fifth Avenue and 84th Street. Pops is a great inventor.

Pops, after Thomas Jefferson, believed that "all men are created equal"—in their necessities, which to his mind are, in order of priority, as follows:

1 potable water, 2 food, 3 shelter, 4 good plumbing, 5 tub baths

Pops set out to alleviate man's suffering by providing said necessities by the simplest means: the Tempwing™ covered shelter, and the Ensuite™, a pop-up toilet, towel rack and tub, covered plumbing and baths.

Pops got most of his ideas from food. He'd thought about papadums and how they bubble and rise in hot oil, then he thought about popovers. It is the Popover™ technology which allowed Pops to develop the Tempwing™.

I slept in a Tempwing™ pod and dreamed that the raccoon, fully clothed, was my guest for dinner.

# CHAPTER
## 4

Jesús Andrade, our doorman, originally from the Dominican Republic, arrived with the pugs and an apology the next morning at seven. He had offered to keep the dogs for us until we "settled in." He had planned to keep them longer, but his wife, it turned out, was allergic.

Usvelia and Gude-
lia arrived at 8:15
from Queens. They
continued to work for
us because their
brother Cresencio
had a lucrative lawn
mowing business and
could support them—
or that's what they
said. I think they

really wanted to keep an eye on Sis and me.

They brought with them a large blue-speckled enamel
cooking pot filled with pink sweet tamales, a popular
Mexican breakfast item.

It was a heavy
breakfast, but given
that it might have
to tide us over until
dinnertime, it was
well received. We

thanked them, and they promised to bring green tamales the next day.

The pugs ran wild until nine, Sis told me later, after which they had to be kept on leashes, in accordance with park regulations. Pops tied the three leashes to his bath- robe belt and mum- bled something about the monks of New Skete handling their dogs this way.

"Yes, but the monks have Ger- man shepherds, not pugs," remarked Mother, as they

each charged in different directions, then spun around
Pops like he was a maypole.

I did what I had done the day before, and would do the next day and every day for a month, maybe longer. I put on my uniform and "went to school."

I had been turned away from the Lycée on that very first day, just as Mother had predicted. But she seemed so happy to think they had let me in that I kept my secret.

I did my "lessons" at the
Met; we were still members.

I wondered what they were doing at the Lycée. I worried about interrupting my education. I didn't want to be like Béni Wurm, who did his *bachot* when he was twenty-two.

I imagined myself taking final exams, and being the old man in the room, with a long beard, a laughingstock.

Sis, on the other hand, delighted in not going to school. She had a reading rock on Pilgrim Hill that looked like a missing bit of Stonehenge. She spent half the day there reading *Tintin* and the other half "scouting for locations." She had a television program in mind, she said, modeled on *The Tonight Show*.

Sis chose a semicircular

marble bench at the west end of her wing as her set. She put on a turtleneck, the uniform of the best TV hosts, and announced that *The Lux-de-Lux Show* would feature the following guests next week: Mary Poppins, Mary Lennox from *The Secret Garden*, Mary (who had a little lamb), Mary (quite contrary), and two other Marys, to be announced.

When I came home around three, Mother was "shoe

shopping," resting her foot on the root of a tree that looked just like a shoe-fitting stool, trying on her old shoes as if they were brand new.

"Shopping is a habit," she said, giving me a stifling hug, "you don't have to break!"

She smelled of nicotine and cologne. Having declared Pops's Smokos to be "the emperor's new cigarettes," she smoked Gauloises.

When she asked me what I had done today at school, I hesitated, then blurted out, "Charlemagne," a good save, and Mother, who could always read me, didn't.

Instead, she left the shoes behind and led me at a clip to the flowerbed in front of the boathouse.

"Notice anything?" she asked. "Look carefully!"

She bent over and pulled a bunch of dark leaves out of the ground, roots and all.

"This," she said, "is silver beet. A.k.a. perpetual spinach!" It had no business being there, she explained, in the midst of the flowers. We spent the rest of the afternoon clearing up the work of guerrilla vegetarians whom Mother blamed for ruining Central Park, declaring with each plant removal that Frederick Olmsted and Calvert Vaux, who had designed the park, were rolling around in their graves.

When Monsieur Marcel arrived that evening, like clockwork and a miracle, Mother handed him a basketful of veggies, which returned to us the next day in the form of crudités with a garlic mayonnaise, and the next, as a mixed-vegetable soufflé.

# CHAPTER
## 5

I'm learning Italian.

This morning at the Met, I followed a group led by a female guide in Italian. I'm going to acquire Japanese too, via osmosis.

Today I came home to the piercing sound of a saxophonist playing "Try to Remember" from *The Fantasticks* under Glade Arch. Mother demanded to see the musician's ID,

telling him it was illegal to play in a public place without a license or an equivalent degree from Juilliard or Berklee College. When he refused to move on, Mother threatened to strike him with her Judith Leiber minaudière, a jeweled handbag in the shape of a panda bear, harder than a rock.

I, however, could do no wrong musically, according to Mother, and was forced to practice the bassoon for forty-five minutes.

At five o'clock our old grandfather clock chimed, but it was nowhere to be found. Because our furniture had been placed around the park almost as it had been at home, when I couldn't find a bookcase or a chair, I just assumed it had been left behind.

"Look up!" cried Sis. "Look up!"

Right above our heads, wedged between two branches at a somewhat odd angle, was our John Berry antique clock. Pops's froggy self-portrait of Diego Rivera that followed you with its eyes hung up there too, as well as the Frida Kahlo, the Siqueiros, and the Warhol. So did the shrunken head from Paraguay. A stuffed sailfish Pops caught in Puerto Vallarta was at the very top of the tree.

We spotted Pops in the distance digging around Pug Hill, uncovering one bottle of wine, and then shaking his head, burying it again, then digging another hole. He did this three or four times until he uncovered what he was

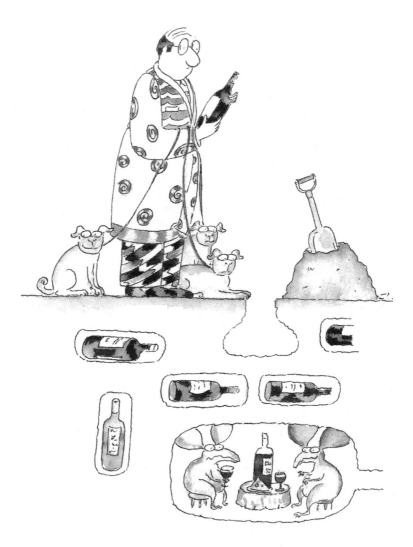

looking for, a cabernet sauvignon. It turned out that Pops's wine cellar was entirely belowground, but he couldn't remember where, exactly.

It was almost bath time, but the maids hadn't arrived to collect Sis. We found Usvelia and Gudelia sitting under a cherry tree, in their stocking feet.

Gudelia held out a circular tin in front of her. She whistled, and down flew a house sparrow and perched on the side of the tin.

The bird removed a folded piece of paper from the tin with its beak, which Gudelia unfolded and read out loud. I was to grow up to be "*un gran abogado*," "a great lawyer," she revealed. The bird picked out a second piece of paper which Usvelia read out to Sis: "*¡Y tú serás una gran actríz, mi cielo!*" "And you will be a great actress, my dear!"

Sis had a tantrum before dinner about her TV show not being real unless it was broadcast, so Pops wired up Sis's studio. She went out "live"

with *The Lux-de-Lux Show*, after her bath, at five-thirty p.m., but it was still a late show, she insisted. Sis signed off with "It's six p.m., do you know where your children are?" Mother keeled over with laughter, and Sis cracked up on air, something she considered most unprofessional.

# CHAPTER
# 6

One evening before dinner, when we were sitting by the pond, Tom Drawbridge, an old friend of Pops's, walked by in his three-piece suit with his briefcase, smoking a cigar.

He walked home from work in midtown this way every day, he explained. Somehow we had missed him. Or perhaps he had avoided us for several weeks

and had taken a different route. Thinking we would be out of the park by now, he returned to his old habit.

He came every day after that, chatted to us for about four minutes, and then went on his way. He was full of news— the Senate, the stock market—news Pops was thirsty for, at first.

Mr. Drawbridge always left his old copy of the *Times* behind by accident, puffy and dotted with circular coffee-cup stains.

Tom had supervised the patent and trademark work on Pops's inventions since the very first, "Oyster Shucking by Suggestion," which wasn't an invention at all but a pamphlet Pops put out when he was sixteen.

If an invention wasn't successful, Tom would return Pops's blueprints to the filing cabinet and say, "Later, 'gator," which signaled to Pops that his invention was before its time, but rest assured, its time would come.

Pops called himself a discoverer, not an inventor. He believed that there was nothing new under the sun, but that we just have to look carefully to uncover what is.

Apart from food, which inspired him, Pops loved Raquel Welch. The ESBB™, acronym for "echo stent and

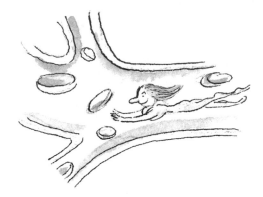

buttress builder," a device that travels through the circulatory system and when met with an obstruction creates a buttress assuring the uninterrupted passage of blood through the vein, was inspired by the actress's performance in *Fantastic Voyage*.

Pops did have a thing about germs. His FrozenScooper™ freeze-dries animal droppings before you pick them up and works in conjunction with the Sh*tShute™, an urban underground system of waste deposit stations and tun-

nels. Surgeons can dip their hands in Glove-Dip™ and be covered by an invisible film so fine it's undetectable to the naked eye, eliminating the need for rubber gloves. The Scrubchamber™, a disinfection booth for surgeons

was discontinued because it destroyed not only outside germs but also the doctors' intestinal flora.

Pops didn't believe that time should be measured absolutely. Never Late Again™, Pops's two-faced watch, shows the official time as well as the time according to one's own perception of time. If you had to be somewhere at three o'clock and you thought that would take fifteen minutes, the watch would put that into real time for you.

POP'S BRAIN

Pops also loved to travel but hated not getting along like a local. He developed Diplomatix™, an effervescent tablet. It comes in "How to Think Like the French" and "How to Think Like the Chinese," among other versions. He hoped one day to tailor the brain tonic beyond cultural boundaries to the personal. "How to Think Like Your Spouse" and "How to Think Like Your Teen" are still in the works.

Because Pops had time on his hands, he spent more time with Mother. Mother said they finally had one thing in common—displacement.

It was more disconcerting than anything else to have
our parents get along so well. We thought the wilderness
had gotten to them and that it was important to get them
back indoors somehow, and back to normal, a.s.a.p.

The dogs, on the other hand, were behaving badly.
They seemed less interested in us, and more interested in
each other, in the pack.

The pugs, who
alternated as guests
and audience members
on Sis's tonight show,
were so uncooperative
one evening, refusing
to wear baby clothes,
growling and even nip-

ping, that Sis had to ask Mother to sit in as her special
guest, Joan of Arc.

The next day, when Pops
was napping, they chewed
through his bathrobe belt and
took off.

"It's the call of the wild,"
Mother explained. We were all
in tears.

# CHAPTER

## 7

"Guinea pigs can't be choosers," said Mother.

Every night either Monsieur Marcel or one of the busboys from the Château Bohème arrived, sometimes with new dishes the chef was trying out on us. Chef Richelieu went for fusion cuisines, French/Peru-

vian, French/Angolan, etc., or "fission cuisines" as Mother referred to them.

We were always grateful, but sometimes we forgot how much. So one Friday evening, when the Château was booked by Doubleday for a private function and packed, they were so busy that they forgot all about us!

We sat staring at the pond. It was really cold. Why were we still having dinner outdoors?

"This is outrageous!" cried Mother.

"No, it's not," said Pops. "We have no reason to expect anything from anybody ever—that's charity for you."

Pops dug up a bottle of Gigondas nevertheless, and Sis produced that morning's pink tamales, which she was saving, one in each pocket, for the squirrels.

Mother and Pops polished off the wine on an empty stomach and became very merry.

"I've been an ass," said Pops. He meant ass as in donkey. Pops didn't swear.

"Now I know what to do!" Pops offered with great enthusiasm. He seemed so pleased with himself that we didn't dare ask what he was talking about, in case we were less enthusiastic than he was.

Going to bed on an empty stomach for the first time in my life was scary.

I wanted to be forty-two and carry a briefcase like Tom Drawbridge, and bring a paycheck home, regular.

# CHAPTER
# 8

The next morning I awoke to find I had mail. Pops had stayed up all night and created a system of pulleys and string via which the four of us could communicate with each other by letter, pod to pod.

Was this his "big idea"?

Pops's letter to me read, "Good morning, Son. I don't think you

should go to school today, I think it's a public holiday. Love, Pops." This was helpful as I no longer kept track of dates.

The Columbus Day Parade turned Pops's study into an echo chamber of float music. "Volare" was followed by "That's Amore," and speeches, all tinny, that came and went as each float went by on Fifth Avenue, above his study.

We didn't go to the parade. With the exception of my trips to the Met, we never left the park. To spend the night in Central Park is to know that it is miles away from the city. It's like going to the Adirondacks or the Hamptons, or Vermont, without the traffic jam. As the sun sets

and you hear
the birds and
then the rats
and other
noises, you are
very far away
from New
York City, and
smack in the
middle of it.

I didn't go
back to
school. From
that day on my lessons seemed pointless, almost silly, trig-
onometry in particular.

I realized that I was in an enchanted forest, or rather
that all woods are enchanted, because the more I looked at
Central Park, the more I saw. And I began to explore
everything around me with a sense of discovery unequaled
by folks like Christopher Columbus or Amerigo Vespucci.

# CHAPTER
# 9

Monsieur Marcel arrived that evening, full of apologies, with a feast to make up for the previous night's missed dinner. He brought Mother a bottle of her favorite dessert wine,
Beaumes de Venise,
a muscat.

Sis thought
Pops's mail system
was a waste of time.
"He should have
done it with birds,"

she said. "Animals will do anything for food, if you ask them nicely."

Sis thought the pugs would be back, but while waiting for their return, had tamed four squirrels.

"How do you do it?" I asked.

"With tamales," she replied.

"I need one more at least," she added, impatiently. "A fifth will play Marmee and double up as Aunt March."

Sis was working on *Little Women*. She had "left television and gone into theater."

She wanted a mixed cast of squirrel, raccoon, and ducks, but that didn't work since they fought, so she stuck to squirrel.

"You can't tame just any squirrel. It has to be the right one. And you never know when he or she will turn up. Casting is all," she explained, going back to her toy sewing machine.

Usvelia had brought her an old embroidered Mexican folkloric costume from the Zandunga dance. It was raggedy, but there were enough good bits of satin and lace to make the *Little Women* wardrobe.

She was dressing the cast in kimonos.

"It's not an artistic statement," Sis explained. "It's just easier if the dresses open at the front."

# CHAPTER
# 10

Pops worked round the clock.

His "big idea" had not been the mailboxes. They were just a warm-up. The real goal was to become "in-suff-pen-dent," as he put it, a combination of self-sufficient and independent.

An elderly Hungarian gentleman, Mr. Hegyessy, who took his constitutional in the park,

ceci n'est pas
du poulet

observed Pops in his labors daily. He appeared to know only one sentence in English: "I love chicken!" which he uttered over and over again.

Pops meant no harm, I'm sure, when he offered Mr. Hegyessy an unsavory-looking gray cube he had "distilled" from the fumes of a barbecue chicken restaurant.

"It's chicken," said Pops.

The old man took a bite.

"It's not chicken," said Mr. Hegyessy, then fainted.

Pops never experimented on anybody but himself after that.

One day we heard a bang from Pops's study, then we saw a large cloud in the shape of a broccoli floret. Pops turned green for a few days.

Two weeks later Pops turned round and hairy and apologized, explaining he'd been working on a coconut recipe.

And another day he looked like a giant walking hamburger for four hours.

Mother had got used to Pops's company, and now she had none.

Mother did her *petit-point* and smoked. She did the *Times* crossword and smoked.

She played solitaire and smoked.

One morning, when the maids arrived, Mother told them to take the day off and go home. They were hesitant, but Mother insisted, telling them it was a national holiday in Argentina.

She wanted to be
alone.

Nobody dressed
for dinner.

Mother looked
daggers at Pops.
"You are so Anglo-
Saxon!" she said.

"Are Jews Anglo-
Saxons?" asked Sis.
They ignored us.

To be too Anglo-
Saxon was Mother's
favorite insult. It
meant that you were

a cold fish instead of being a fiery Latin, an Argentine
firecracker, like she was.

# CHAPTER
## 12

521 hours later, Pops emerged from his study and said, "Ta-dah!" uncovering The Horn o' Plenty™, that would make us in-suff-pen-dent, he said, for good.

The Horn o' Plenty™, or HOP™ for short, looked like a crockpot with an antenna. It had a dial you could set to breakfast, lunch, or dinner, and also a button to choose from a numbered list of restaurants in the

B L D

RESTAURANT

○ (SANT AMBROEUS)

GUESTS

5

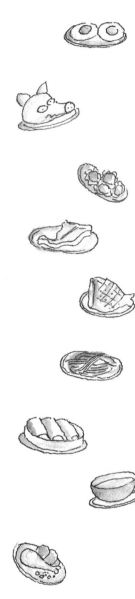

vicinity: 1) Maxwell's Plum, 2) Sant Ambroeus, 3) Choc Full o' Nuts, among others.

You set the dial to the meal required, then entered the restaurant of your choice, and then the number of people you had to feed. The HOP™, through a system of radar and whatnot, extracted a meal from the fumes emanating from French toast, or bacon—anything on the stove—and some salads, if they contained onion.

The HOP™ had one major drawback, which was that you could not order à la carte. You had to take whatever it served up, so the meal was always a surprise.

When Monsieur Marcel arrived that evening with the
aluminum foil swans, Pops appeared in a white chef's
outfit.

"You look like a dentist," said Mother.

Pops unveiled the HOP™ and served up a steamy
bouillabaisse.

"You forgot the bibs," said Mother.

Pops had dug up two bottles of Sancerre and we kids were allowed a bit of wine mixed with water for the occasion.

Monsieur Marcel correctly identified the bouillabaisse, which was from one of our favorite restaurants, Le Veau d'Or. When Pops explained to him how the HOP™ worked, Monsieur Marcel dropped his spoon into the bowl with a splash, turned very red in the face, and then very pale, almost white.

"You'll put me out of beezness," he said, almost in tears. "Technology will destroy us all!"

Pops assured him that the restaurant experience is incomparable to any other, and that he was in no danger, but Monsieur Marcel left before dessert.

"My eye, my eye!" I heard Pops cry out later that evening, when I was on the way to my quarters. I ran back to find Pops whimpering, holding his hand over one eye. Mother stood a few feet away from him holding a mallet from Sis's toy croquet set.

"You're such a baby," said Mother and headed to her pod. "I didn't do anything to him." She slammed the door, though we hadn't any.

# CHAPTER
# 13

Mother was still mad at Pops for ignoring her while he was working on his invention.

"Well, he didn't exactly reinvent the wheel," she barked, "or grow hair!" It was Pops's Achilles heel. He had developed a cream to grow hair once, but the hair that resulted was curly and unruly. Mother christened it "the Elliott Gould," and it went right back into the filing cabinet.

One evening, Pops, in an effort to impress Mother, added brandy to the HOP™, which was full of crêpes suzette, and set them alight with a wooden match. The result was a fierce explosion, which sent us all flying in four different directions.

What we did not know at the time was that at the Mark Hotel, where the dessert was from, there was also a fierce explosion in the kitchen.

Usvelia and Gudelia arrived the next morning to dinner things on the ground, and the four of us passed out in front of the pond. Our hair was singed and our faces black,

like coal miners. It was necessary to use the yellow emergency phone in Sis's wing to call 911.

Our injuries were superficial, said the paramedics, but Pops, who had been closest to the HOP™ when it exploded, was in bad shape. He had no eyebrows to speak of.

He refused to be taken to the hospital for observation. Instead, Usvelia and Gudelia treated Pops's skin with egg whites, shaved almonds, and finally mint leaves, Mexican remedies. He slept soundly for the rest of the day. The HOP™ remained intact.

While Pops was asleep, an old friend, Hamid Kohlrabi, ran into Mother. He was walking his whippets. My parents knew him from the racetrack, when we had Heliocentric and Scintilla, and a few other racehorses.

Hamid wore long robes like Lawrence of Arabia but looked more like Johnny Carson. He was in the furniture business.

Hamid came the next day, and the next. His skinny
dogs made me miss our fatty pugs.

One afternoon I followed Mother and Hamid on their walk into the woods. They sat at a picnic table. Hamid produced an insulated Chinese basket with a teapot in it, and two cups. They had tea with *savoiardi*, a.k.a. ladyfingers, the lightest biscuit in the world.

Just before they parted, Hamid gave Mother a small round box of crystallized violets.

# CHAPTER
## 14

Mother did not come to dinner the next day. I had seen her earlier wearing a Valentino. She looked more beautiful than ever.

Pops kept adding restaurants to the HOP™'s repertoire. He had just added the Mansion Diner at York Avenue and 86th Street, and we got

challah French toast and hot fudge sundaes for dinner. Sis was ecstatic.

I ate very slowly, thinking that any minute now Mother would be back—that if I drew out the meal, she wouldn't miss it. She'd be late, but she'd still be home for dinner.

Pops headed uphill to his study before dessert. Sis and I went for a walk. We had never been for a walk so late in the evening, or walked so far.

We headed north, to a green lawn beside the Met. Through the large floor-to-ceiling windows we could see the Temple of Dendur, all lit up. There was a party going on, dancing at one end of the hall and dining at the other. The floral arrangements were too big. A waiter spotted us and tapped on the window, shooing us away.

"This is so Dickens," said Sis. We moved along but kept snooping. We crouched down on the grass.

There were men in black tie, women in long gowns and . . . Mother!

"Mother's the belle of the ball," sighed Sis. She did look lovelier than anybody else at the party.

Hamid looked good too, in a tux. Mother looked happy and carefree. She had not looked so happy for some time.

That night I couldn't get to sleep
until I knew Mother was home safely.
Finally I heard noises.

I heard Mother say, "Go to hell!" and
Pops reply, "Well, it's a lot warmer
there." It was one of their favorite verbal
volleys and I dozed off almost immediately. If I had not
been so tired I might have realized this fight was different.

# CHAPTER
## 15

The next day, very early—the birds were just waking up—I heard a gallop. I ran out of my pod and saw a man on horseback in white robes. He'd ridden into the park at 79th Street, just below the Met.

I ran after him, only to see him ride up the hill to Mother's wing and whisk her away.

"So much for high

drama," said Sis, who had been awakened by the clippity-
clop past her wing and caught them as they exited at 72nd
and Fifth.

"They put the horse in a trailer and drove away in a
stretch. So Euro-trashy!" added Sis.

"Did your Mother leave a note?" asked Pops.

Mother didn't leave a note.

"I saw her writing a note last night," I lied. "I saw her fold the note, open the mailbox, and then a wind came up . . ."

"Yes, a wind came up," Sis came to my rescue, "and a goose ate it."

Pops walked over to the north side of the pond, pulled out Mother's bottle of cologne, untied it, threw the foo dog back into the pond, climbed up

the Alice in Wonderland statue, and emptied the bottle of
cologne on Alice's head.

"It's like a shampoo," said Sis.

Those were the last words spoken that day, by any of us, except that I did explain to Usvelia and Gudelia what had happened when they arrived. Then I told them it was a national holiday in Argentina, and they went home.

# CHAPTER
# 16

The maids moved in.

Usvelia and Gudelia arrived with sixteen suitcases and
some of their furniture
covered in plastic.

Pops was so grateful
for their presence that he
attempted something he
had not tried before, television reception.

The sisters lived for
their *telenovela*, which
was in its last episodes. It

was enough of a sacrifice for the sisters to stay with us, but we could not let them miss their show.

Pops unveiled the brand-new feature he'd just developed at dinner. Not only were the sisters able to order steaks, but Pops even asked how they would like these done, a first, and provided three sauces on the side.

Sis had a baked potato with butter, sour cream, and chives.

At 9 p.m., *El Derecho de Nacer* appeared on an oversized dishcloth stretched between two trees. In one sitting we were hooked.

# CHAPTER
# 17

Pops, Sis, and I spent most of the time indoors, alone in our pods.

Pops ate.

Pops had been obese as a child. His parents sent him to summer fat camp in Vermont and he had not looked back. But some problems never leave you entirely.

Pops fine-tuned his machine to deliver junk food.

When Usvelia and Gudelia were through picking up Twinkie, Ho Ho and Ding Dong wrappers in Pops's pod, they sewed two pairs of Pops's pajamas into one, and two bathrobes. He had doubled in size, exactly.

One afternoon, at five, the sisters beckoned us all to leave our pods for a BIG surprise. The trees around the pond, now bare, were decorated with red, green, and silver bulbs. They had transformed the Hans Christian Ander-

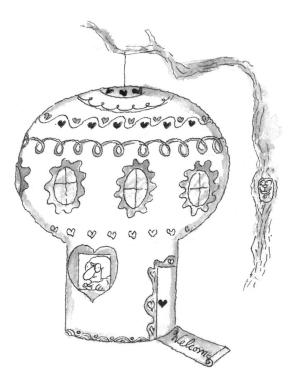

sen statue into a Nativity scene. The bronze duck was one
of the animals in the stable, Hans Christian Andersen was
Balthazar, one of the Three Kings, and his top hat was the
manger, and a scantily clad doll
on top of it the Baby Jesus.

Was it almost Christmas?

That night, strained beyond
its capacity servicing Pops's
gluttony, the HOP™ gave out.

# CHAPTER
# 18

The next morning there was no breakfast, nor water in the pond.

Overnight, the pond had been drained. At the bottom it was sludge mixed with broken pieces of rock and glass and concrete that took a few days to dry out.

Sis, who expected the water removal to reveal a version of Nessie, the

Loch Ness monster, swallowed her disappointment and announced that the spot was "perfect for Beckett."

Pops, who normally wouldn't have noticed, bemoaned the loss of his water view. He sat on the edge of the pond, his feet dangling in his double pajama pants, then jumped into the mud when something caught his eye, finishing off his needlepoint slippers.

It was Mother's foo dog. He stared at it for a minute, then picked it up and cradled it like a baby. He started to cry and didn't stop. It had finally dawned on him that he had lost Mother.

Usvelia and Gudelia tried to distract us by teaching us how to make a traditional Christmas piñata, in the shape of a seven-pointed star.

"Each point in the star represents one of the deadly sins," said Gudelia, not mentioning that the fruit and candies and peanuts that come out of a broken piñata represent blessings and redemption for those same sins, because she didn't want to talk about food. But the seven cones we

made, the points of the star, reminded Sis of ice cream cones, and she said so.

As soon as it was dark, Sis and I put on Mother and Pops's old Beatles' wigs and snuck out of the Park to find pretzels, and Mother.

# CHAPTER
## 19

We hoped we had the right address.

But as we climbed up the five stories of the town house
on East 77th Street
thanks to one of Pops's
earlier inventions, the
Abseilpatch™, we knew
we were in the right
place.

The higher we went,
the more Western furni-
ture gave way to Middle
Eastern decoration.

Though the lights were on, the house appeared to be empty until we got to the very top floor, where it was all carpets.

A boy and a girl sat inside alone, reading at opposite ends of the room. The boy, about my age, had an Eton crop, and the little girl, about Sis's age, had black hair pulled back into tight braids.

"Hamid's kids! They're living like genies in a bottle, how fab," said Sis with a hint of envy.

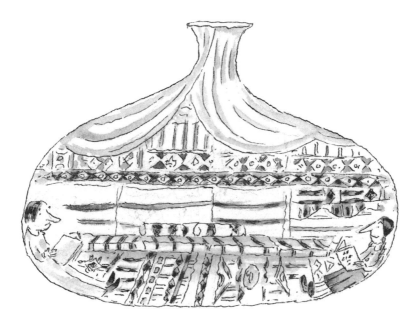

A phone rang and the boy answered.

"Is that you, Papa?" He turned to his sister. "It's papa!" he said, and she ran over and tried to pull the phone away from her brother unsuccessfully.

"When will you be home from Buenos Aires? Uh-huh . . . uh-huh. We're fine . . . She's right here, I'll put her on. Bye, Papa."

The little girl spoke to her father. When she hung up, she made an announcement.

"He's coming home. *She's* still with him."

"That woman?"

"Well, I'm not going to call a stranger 'Mother,'" said the boy.

"Neither am I. She smokes like a chimney!"

"They're talking about Mother," Sis cried out. We had our noses right up to the glass windows.

"Bang!" The window shook and we were face to face with Hamid's two ferocious whippets. They pressed their slender paws into the window and scratched with overgrown nails, and barked. We were too stunned to move.

Next, the two children's faces appeared right opposite ours, on the other side of the glass. It was like looking in a mirror. They looked a little sad, like us.

Were it not for the dark hair, they might have been doppelgangers.

I grabbed hold of Sis, slid down the side of the town house too fast, and landed in a ceramic planter, which broke in two.

We ran home like nobody's business. They hadn't missed us. Usvelia and Gudelia were watching their *telenovela*, Pops was still crying. There was just one difference—the pugs were back!

# CHAPTER
# 20

I think you can get used to anything, except the cold. The pugs came home, I'm sure, because they smelled snow.

At about noon the sky became as gray as the bottom of our dry pond. Sis was rehearsing Phoebe as the lead, Winnie, in *Happy Days*, "a thankless role," she explained.

A light snow began to fall. Sis was so happy to have the

pugs back and not to have to work with squirrels anymore, she didn't notice.

The snow stuck, and the flakes got heavier and fell in
gobs which surprisingly sat lightly on the ground. We
were forced indoors. The pugs and
I piled into Sis's pod.

Neither of us mentioned what
was really on our minds, that we
had been replaced by children with
darker hair, Hamid's ready-made
family. But for the snow falling,

everything was still, and silent, the only sound being an occasional whimper from Pops.

"He'll fill the pond if he keeps going," I thought, "and we'll have an ice skating rink."

Sis and the pugs were fast asleep.

In the middle of the night I let the pugs out. They would only do their business on the west side of the pond, in an area of brush south of the Hans Christian Andersen

statue. I bent down to clean up after Sancho, and when I looked up I saw a furry white figure walking toward me from the East Drive. Was it the yeti?

I didn't think there could be a yeti in North America. The abominable snowman, I was convinced, lived in the Himalayas, in Tibet.

When the creature got within ten feet of me, it stopped.
I remembered that you are not supposed to run from a
bear and some wildcats, so I stood still.

As it was after midnight, the pugs were off leash. Sancho ran toward the creature and, afraid Phoebe and Olive
would follow, I crouched down and held tight onto both of
them by the collar.

The creature picked Sancho up with one paw, then
began to walk toward me. I picked up the two pugs and
ran for my life.

# CHAPTER
## 21

The next morning, by the time I got up, the snow had stopped. The empty pond now looked like a clean white pool, instead of a gray mess. All the edges of the sidewalk, of the steps, had been softened. It was like a living room, all curves, no angles.

Usvelia and Gudelia's brother Cresencio arrived with an enamel pot of red chilaquiles topped with cream, hot coffee, and five pairs of

cross-country skis for us. He said he would bring green chilaquiles next time.

Sis was worried that Santa Claus wouldn't come because we had no chimney. I told her that he would, and, appeased, she took off with Usvelia and Gudelia on skis. Pops was too sad to go and I used that as my pretext for staying behind.

Equipped with Mother's binoculars, I took off on foot

to find Sancho. By now the yeti's tracks had been snowed over. There was nothing to follow.

It wasn't until after dark that Sis noticed Sancho was missing. I had looked everywhere, and I was too tired to make anything up, so I told her what had happened the night before.

Sadly resigned to the idea that Sancho had been eaten, we left the pugs behind in Sis's pod at about eight. We dug a trench just below the Central Park Loop where I had seen the creature, and filled it with snow. We also suspended a large net from the trees, borrowing pulleys from Pops's mail system. We waited for the yeti.

Sis had insisted on an early warning system, in case we fell asleep at our watchpost. We were woken by the little bell, then a cry as our victim fell into the trench with a thud and the net covered the hole in a split second.

I was afraid to look, so Sis leaned over the hole first.

Pulling the net away she exclaimed, "That's no monster! That's Mother!"

# CHAPTER
## 22

Fortunately there were no broken bones. Mother was wearing a full-length white ermine coat, with matching hat, gloves, and boots. She could easily have been mistaken for the yeti. She had Sancho in her arms. He had not been eaten after all.

Mother didn't want to wake Pops. She wanted "quality time" with Sis and me, so we all piled into Sis's pod. We were packed in like sardines but we were warm as toast.

The maids, who had prayed

for Mother's prompt return, lighting candles to Santa Elena de la Cruz, were not as surprised the next morning to see Mother as we had been.

Still, both Usvelia and Gudelia broke into tears, then packed and sped off to Queens.

S<sup>TA</sup> ELENA DE LA CRUZ

Sis and I took off on skis and left Mother to deal with Pops, and vice versa.

Sis said she was worried that Mother wouldn't love Pops anymore now that he wasn't his handsome self, which is when I realized that Pops had not been good-looking to begin with. He had lost a bit of weight since the HOP gave out, but not enough. It was possible that Mother might not be there when we got back.

But she was.

When we arrived at four, Mother was there, and so was Monsieur Marcel, with a *bûche de Noël*, the traditional

French Christmas cake in the shape of a log, decorated with marzipan mushrooms. Pops looked swell.

It was Christmas Eve.

There was some distress in the night caused by indigestion, given the rich meal, but after that we slept like logs.

# CHAPTER
## 23

The next morning we woke up back in Penthouse B. Everything was in its place, as it always had been.

Santa Claus came, even though we haven't a chimney.

Mother gave Pops a wardrobe in his new portly size, which fit perfectly. "I should have been a spy," said Mother, and winked. I found out that while she was away Mother had visited us in the park daily, without our knowledge, except when she took that trip to Buenos Aires.

There was a knock at the door.

"Ho, ho, ho!" It was Tom Drawbridge dressed as Santa Claus but carrying the same briefcase as usual.

He handed Pops a manila envelope full of diagrams and paperwork.

"Waste Knot™, want not!" he said.

"Waste Knot™, want not," replied Pops, removing his glasses to wipe away tears. Then he blew his nose with a honk.

"You old S.O.B.!" Mother wiped away the rest of Pops's tears and gave him a hug and a huge kiss.

The Waste Knot™, a device that captures wasted energy, both

physical and emotional, from the atmosphere and recycles it into an effective fuel, was Pops's latest and, as it turned out, his greatest invention.

He'd got the idea when struggling to open a vacuum-sealed leg of lamb three years earlier. He was ready to marinate the leg in garlic, rosemary, mustard,

and champagne, but he could not get the leg out of its packaging. Unable to find the kitchen scissors, he pulled at the sealed plastic with his hands, only managing to stretch the plastic but not to tear it.

Exasperated, Pops

finally took to the plastic
with his teeth.

This expenditure of
energy, both physical and
emotional, outweighed the
result, he thought, of
releasing the leg of lamb
from its packaging, i.e.
was a waste of energy.

He thought of how many times a day a human wastes
energy. If only that misspent energy could be captured
somehow, and be made useful.

Pops poured our fortune into developing the Waste
Knot™. When that sum didn't suffice, he borrowed and
borrowed. When a major investor pulled out, we sank.

But the week before last,
a new investor, Moritz
Hegyessy, had picked up
the slack. Pops was in business again.

After lunch, Sis
announced that *Happy Days*
wasn't Christmassy

enough, but that she had prepared "a brand-new post-prandial presentation." She had received a Victorian toy theater from Santa and was through working with animals, even domesticated ones.

"There's no place like home," said Pops as he emerged from his bedroom in a second new suit, and another gift from Mother, a toupée.

"No, there's no place like home," said Mother, blowing cigarette smoke through her nose, sipping a rum toddy.

"No, there's no place like home," said Sis, cutting the cast of *A Child's Christmas in Wales* out of cardboard.

"No, there's no place like home," we all repeated, as we headed downstairs and across Fifth Avenue, back to the pond.

## THE END.

# ACKNOWLEDGMENTS

To Huguette Martel, my thanks for your enthusiasm since I began talking about this story seventeen years ago. Without your friendship and support, and your distinguished eye that not only detects four-leaf clovers, this book would not exist.

Susan Lyons, thank you for reading the manuscript and giving me brilliant guidance and encouragement.

Jennifer Koontz, thank you for providing a safety net for the finished manuscript. I am forever grateful for your patience, generosity, and attention to detail.

To Michael Sternberg and Donna Green, thanks for your unflinching faith in my work.

Also to Jane Nicholls, many thanks for even more unflinching faith and calling me "a writer" in an email.

Thanks to WNYC, my live-in companion forevermore.

To my mother Inés Roth, I am sorry you are not on earth to see this. It is your story and I know that you and Lil and Herminia can see this from where you are. You didn't insist I go to law school or study marine biology at Scripps but bought me large books about Saul Steinberg and Gertrude Stein, and encouraged every ounce of talent I have. I finally have my own American book. Thank you.

To the Benjamins, my step-family for too short a time, may you all remember Robert S. Benjamin fondly through this book. To Robert and Audrey Benjamin, thanks for being my New York family.

Finally, a special thanks to Alan Benjamin, my brother, who has his heart in the right place, for inspiring the character of the narrator and allowing me to name him after him. It is an honor. Or, as we say, "es un honor."

And to Central Park, which saves us all.


Victoria Roberts